CHRIS LOWRY

Everglades Zombie

Contents

1

EVERGLADE ZOMBIE

"I need a hero," she sang under her breath as she wiped the gunk off his face.

"You should probably hold out for the morning light," he said to her.

She felt like laughing but held it in. He could tell. He could always tell with her.

He reached up with a grungy hand and held the side of her face. She leaned into it.

Her mother had held her cheek like that, just the presence of it made her feel calm.

"You need a bath," she said.

She took his hand away from her face and fought down the reluctance, missed the soothing feel of his warmth next to hers.

She bathed it in the bloody water in the pan, wiping the crimson rag up and down the wrinkles, scars and bruises.

There were more of them. Always more of them.

"Are you going out again?"

She couldn't look at him when she asked. She knew the answer. They hadn't found his daughter yet, his youngest. He would keep going.

She was afraid that one time, he wouldn't come back.

"In the morning," he groaned.

She pushed him back into the rough pillow made from a folded comforter in the back of the bus.

"Sleep," she told him. "I'm going to help Peg."

He closed his eyes and laid back on the simple white sheet folded over their bag. He would sleep, then later, after he woke, she would burn it.

It wouldn't be the first one. She suspected nor the last either.

She left him the bus and stepped into the afternoon. The heat and mugginess was growing thick, a sign they were getting further South.

They had found her in the panhandle of Florida, so she was familiar with the feeling, but she had never been much further South than Jacksonville.

"How is he?" Brian looked up from the fire.

"He'll live," she smirked.

It was a private joke among them. He, of all of them, probably would live.

They had called him Z-proof, behind his back, as well as other choice names. Asshole. Stubborn. Jackass. They were all favorites.

Sometimes they were said with an underlying current of love.

Peg looked over at the three people huddled on the far side of the fire.

"Think they were worth it?" she said in a low voice.

"Were we?" Brian asked.

She picked up a stick and poked the embers around a pot of boiling beans.

"We're running low on food," said Peg. "Water. He was supposed to bring those back."

Brian patted her knee.

"We'll stretch it," he said and patted his thin stomach. "I've been meaning to drop a few lbs anyway."

She didn't smile back at him. Being back in Florida made her nervous. Hell, it made them all nervous.

Orlando had almost five million people before the zombie apocalypse wiped out the population. But instead of leaving dead bodies to quickly decay in the fetid heat, they turned Z and roamed the countryside.

Anna imagined them bouncing back and forth between the Atlantic and the Gulf, a wide swath of herding Z forever walking between the two sides of the peninsula.

"What's so funny?" Peg snapped.

"Us," she said.

"Funny in the head," Brian said.

Anna nodded. She picked up two bowls of beans, meager portions carefully measured into fifteen almost equal servings and took them to the huddled trio.

"Hi," she said. "I'm Anna."

"Raymer," the oldest said.

He held out a callused black hand and took the food from her.

"Thank you," he passed one to the woman and the other to the teen.

Anna grabbed two more bowls and returned to join them.

"Julie," he introduced the woman as he accepted his food from her. "And Louise."

"Lou," said the girl with large black eyes that glimmered in the firelight. "I like to be called Lou."

"Lou," Raymer stuttered. "I forget."

Anna spooned up a couple of beans at a time, stretching it out to make it last.

The canned white beans were mostly flavorless, but the salt and pepper Peg added competed to dominate the soupy mess.

It didn't last long enough, and Anna wondered if it was just enough food to keep her hungry.

"What happened out there?" she asked, setting aside her empt bowl.

They would clean it later. All of them, and pack them away for breakfast tomorrow. The last of the oatmeal.

Raymer stared into his empty dish as if wishing would make it full again. He had saggy skin and baggy eyes, the look of a man who lost weight too fast.

His gray pallor told her he was either sick or starving, and for a moment, she wondered if it was both.

"Are you bit?" she asked.

He shook his head.

"None of us," he said. "But we haven't eaten in days. I'm lightheaded."

He rocked next to the woman in front of the fire, Julie, who ate in silence and never looked up.

Lou, on the other hand, finished her food fast, and watched the others eat like a puppy ready to beg. Or ready to dart in to snatch any scraps that might fall.

"We had a house," Raymer said.

He stared into the fire as Brian fed branches into the flames, building it against the growing darkness.

"It wasn't our house, but we were making it home. At first, there were more of us. Eight," he said with pride.

"The house was empty of people when we found it, and the others joined us. That's how we met Louise."

"Lou," the girl corrected.

"Lou. We had some food, we had a garden in back, a couple of weapons. Most of all, we had a fence. The fence kept us safe."

Julie stared in the flames with him, as if the fire was a televisions screen casting back an image of their new found home.

"Routine," said Raymer. "We settled into one pretty quick. Two people hunting, three to scavenge, and the rest tended the house."

He motioned to the tiny campsite. There were two tents set up on the roof of the bus, a couple of folding chairs by the fire, but the majority of their sleeping and living space was inside the grimy yellow bus.

"We made it work," he said.

"Much like we do," Anna told him and he nodded.

"It's the way now."

"But you're not home now," said Peg.

Anna noticed she hand sharpened the end of the stick, scraping it on one of the rocks that ringed the fire. She lifted the point and examined it, set it back in the coals to harden the tip.

"One of our people got bit. He knew what was going to happen, but he hid it from us."

"You didn't notice him get sick?" Brian said.

Julie sniffled and hid her face. Raymer patted her on the shoulder and drew her close.

"We had a cold run through the house," he said. "Something so simple before all of this began. A fever. The sniffles. We used to call it a twenty four hour bug, though every time I caught it, it lasted for about three days. This one was no exception."

"We thought he got it last," said Lou. "He went to his room and laid down with a fever. We thought he had a cold."

Raymer sighed.

"Like I said, there were eight of us in the house. The three bedrooms were like dorms. He bit the two in the room with him while they slept. When we opened the door to check on him the next morning, he bit another. We got out and ran."

"Into?"

"Him," Raymer nodded toward the bus. "Lou tripped and one was about to grab her. I ran back to help, but I was too slow."

"He saved me," said Lou. "Came sprinting in like a marathon runner."

She slapped her hands together.

"Whack. Whack. Splat," she demonstrated. "He got the four of them in like three seconds."

"He does that," said Brian. "Saved all of us."

"A lot of practice," Anna added.

"So he killed the four people from your house," she pointed as she counted. "But I'm only counting three."

"Our man who was bit."

"His name was Jonathan," said Lou.

"Jonathan," Raymer rubbed his face. "Jonathan must have forgotten to cover his tracks, or maybe he was in a haze when he was bitten. He led a big group of them right to us."

"They heard our screaming," said Lou. "They came out of the woods. We were surrounded."

Peg and Brian exchanged a look with Anna.

"How many?"

"Two or three dozen," said Raymer.

He looked at the windows on the bus.

"He killed them all," he whispered.

2

CHAPTER TWO

Something that used to bother me about zombie movies and tv shows. Not that they were unrealistic. I mean, come on, they were about the dead walking.

Until they weren't make believe anymore. Like Star Trek and all the incredible devices Science Fiction promised us for the future.

We were supposed to have flying cars, and robot dogs. Instead, we got Z.

But in movies, the people would have a flat tire or something like it. They would get out of the car and not check their surroundings.

Then the Z would sneak up on them.

Are you kidding me?

Then they would fight, but the simple effort of pushing the Z back, of keeping it from snapping them, would exhaust them. The fighter could barely lift their arms.

Their bare, uncovered arms.

It made no sense. Maybe it was done for dramatic effect, but for me, it just made the suspension of disbelief all the harder.

"We keep covered," I explained to the group.

They probably felt like it was the thousandth time and I'd tell them a thousand more, just so it sunk in. Second nature.

I remember reading a book about a man who contracted leprosy in the modern world. He was taught to do a constant self assessment because of the way the disease worked. If he got a sore, or a cut, he couldn't feel it, and it would progress or advance until pieces started to fall off of him.

He even yelled at people for touching him. He wanted to be safe and be sure.

We were like that.

Or we were supposed to be.

"Two layers," I held up two fingers. "More if you can handle it."

"But it's hot," said Byron.

"You'll get used to it. And if you get bit, you'll get a fever even hotter. Then you're dead."

The kid mopped his brow with a rag damp from sweat.

We were all sweating. And it was not comfortable.

"Pants, tucked or taped to your boots. No exposed skin. Thick canvas fabric works good."

"Like work pants," said Brian.

"Or denim," Peg added.

"Yes," I said. "The movies, they would run around in shorts and tank tops. Or the zombies would bite through blue jeans. That's not the the case. They don't have supernatural strength. Their bite is going to hurt. It's going to bruise, but if they can't get through the cloth, you won't get sick. You won't turn."

"How do you know?" Raymer asked.

"Has it happened?" Julie added.

I looked around at Brian, Peg. Moved over to Anna, and Byron.

They shook their heads.

"I think we don't take the risks," I said.

"WE don't take the risks," said Brian. "You do stupid stuff all the time."

The light giggles sounded from around the circle.

"It's my modus operendi," I said. "I'm kind of an expert at making dumb moves."

"But you're here," said Anna.

"And I cover up. We cover up. We check our surroundings. It's a mantra."

They nodded. I don't know if they got it. But some of them did. Some of it got through.

When I was growing up, they sent a fire marshal to the elementary school to talk about what to do if you caught on fire.

Stop. Drop and roll.
   So easy, so simple and it stuck. Like the lyrics to a song so hard to forget, it pops up at the weirdest time.

Stop. Drop and roll.

"One hundred. Three sixty," I tried it out.

"What's that?" Lou asked.

"One hundred percent coverage. Look around you three hundred and sixty degrees. One hundred. Three Sixty."

I grinned at Brian.

"Very clever," he deadpanned.

"You work on that all night?" Peg asked.

"Found it online," I said.

"I miss the internet," Lou sighed.

"We miss a lot," Brian stared at the group.

Being back in Florida was doing something to him, causing him to retreat into his shell. He had wanted to build a safe community, had wanted to fort up and be a leader.

It hadn't worked out the way he planned. There were stronger men out there, armed men, and he made a couple of decisions that put him under their thumb.

Crossing back into the sunshine state had left him depleted somehow. As if his energy came from moving North.

"That's what I'm trying to teach us," I said. "Reinforce the message. We don't want to miss anything. Being covered. Staying alert."

They nodded again.

"NSB is an island," I told them. "We don't know what we're going to find. It could be a haven. It could be a haven for the Z."

I glanced at the buildings across the water. A collection of older two story condominiums built in the seventies to capture snowbirds for their yearly migration to warmer climes.

Eight buildings. All empty by the look of them, but I knew that was deceiving. Each unit could have Z in it.

They could be herded over by the beach chasing seagulls. They could be on the far end of the island.

There was no way to tell from here, except it looked deserted.

The island was seven miles long from the tip at the inlet, all the way down to the long stretch of sandy beach and marsh on the border of the Space Coast.

A thousand houses. Two thousand plus condos. A lot of ground for a scared little girl to hide in.

But Bis was smart. Way smarter than me. She left a sign back at the refugee camp to tell me which direction to go.

She would leave another.

"Tomorrow morning," I said. "We dress. We look around to make sure it's safe. Then we go."

"Are we leaving someone here to guard the bus?" Byron asked.

I glanced at Brian.

"You said we don't split up."

"That settles it," Byron said and checked the chamber on his rifle.

I continued to stare at the conclave across the river, wondered what the morning might bring.

River dolphins breached off the water in front of us and I smiled.

Bem, Anna and Karen moved to the edge of the boardwalk that ran alongside the river, kept their awes in check but watched in fascination.

"They're good luck," I thought, but kept it to myself.

We were going to need all the luck we could get.

3

CHAPTER THREE

There was no plan. No effort at a proper escape.

There was only too many of them, and not enough of us.

Guns jutted from their grouping like pins on a porcupine. Aimed at the sky. Aimed at us. Around us even.

"Don't move!" one of them screamed.

Like we would even consider it. There were five of them for every one of us.

But they way they were grouped was stupid. Too close together, like they were a phalanx instead of a unit. Great formation against spears and maybe even Z.

They could shoot in every direction.

But bad news against a machine gun.

"I said don't move!" the one in the front screamed again.

Which was weird. None of us were moving.

"When I say, duck," I said out of the side of my mouth.

My people dropped.

"I didn't say," I shouted as I stood all by myself.

"Down!" screamed Brian.

I dropped on top of him, ignored the wheeze that exploded out of him.

He gagged as I yanked his rifle by the strap and used him like a tripod.

A squirming, mewling tripod.

The bullets ripped into the tight grouping of men facing us. Brian had it set on full auto, which I told him not to do.

He never listened and this time I was glad for it.

The front row of the group dropped, as the middle tried to push back. I raked them again before they could recover and respond.

Then they did.

Their aim was off.

Mine was not.

Their shots chewed up the asphalt in front of us, digging up geysers of chunky grit that bounced across us.

Brian screamed. Peg screamed. Maybe some more.

But someone beside me started shooting from the ground, and then on the other side and the group in front of us disintegrated and turned to run.

There is no nobility in shooting a man in the back when he is running away from a fight.

Nobility is overrated.

I rolled off Brian, held out my hand for the hunting rifle the Boy was using.

"Gimme," I said and scooted up to one knee.

I lined up on the farthest, the one who looked like he was going in a straight line and dropped.

I got six more before they figured out what was happening and skedaddled into side roads.

"Shit," I said.

Brian sat up and wiped asphalt off his face.

"Why?" he asked.

"Survivor troubles," I said.

"Don't stop believing," he said.

"Wrong band," I stood up and held out my hand to help him up.

"Really? What am I thinking of?"

"Eye of the Tiger."

"Right," he glanced at the group. "Anyone hurt?"

Everyone chimed in. No hits. No injuries.
I herded us off the road and into a driveway, in case the survivors of our encounter decided payback was in order and took a turkey shoot down the roadway.

"This is no good," I muttered watching the street.

Raymer looked at the dead bodies contorted in the road.

"I'd say half is good," he whispered.

"That means half are still out there," said Brian. "He means they'll hunt us."

"Will they?"

I nodded.

"I would."

"This is going to make a house to house search harder," said the Boy.

"Should we go back? Split up?" Bem said.

"We stay together."

It came out harsher than I meant.

"Sorry," I said.

"Geez Dad, you don't have to say it. I know how you are when you get scared."

She punched me in the shoulder.

"That's him scared?" Lou whispered to Raymer loud enough to hear.

"Shoot," said Peg. "You should see him when he's terrified. He probably would have gotten them all."

I shook my head.

"I got lucky," I said.

"He gets lucky a lot," said Peg.

"Yeah he does," Brian said in a perverted voice that drew a few laughs. Nervous laughs.

"Next house over," I said. "We go in, lay low. At least until we figure out the next move."

I didn't wait for their nods. I led them around the side of the driveway we were in, and across the green strip that separated the houses.

"You said next house," Brian said as we passed the first two by, slinking from yard to yard.

I stopped at a two story home and tried the door.

"I wanted elevation," I told him.

The door was unlocked and opened to an empty home. It had that feel, and smell. Not dead, but stale.

Unused.

I stepped back and ushered everyone through the door the closed it behind us.

4

CHAPTER FOUR

The front room stretched from the bay window overlooking the street to a wall of sliding glass doors in a family room in the back.

The two rooms bracketed a kitchen, with stairs along the opposite wall that led to the bedrooms.

The furniture in the front room was scooted against the windows, scratches on the hardwood from where it had been moved.

"Check the kitchen," Brian said and moved with Raymer to inspect the cabinets.

"With me," I said to Tyler.

He readied his rifle and followed me up the stairs. I almost told the Boy to stay, but he dropped in behind Tyler and moved up with us.

There were two small bedrooms to the left of the landing, and a master on the rear that overlooked the back yard.

All were empty, though the beds were messed up. Clothes were scattered in front of the closet, like someone had packed in a hurry.

I moved to the French doors in the master bedroom and peeked out into the backyard.

The view was better, but still didn't give me enough information. I could see over several of the surrounding houses, but nothing moved.

Everything looked deserted, which we knew wasn't true.

Maybe they were hiding.

"Anything?" the Boy breathed next to me.

I shook my head.

"Keep watch," I told him. "Get me if you see something."

I motioned to the front bedroom that overlooked the street.

"Same," Tyler said and moved to the side of the window.

I left them to watch and slipped back down the stairs.

"Anything?" Brian asked.

"No."

"Nothing here either," he said. "Not a good place to call home."

"They emptied it out," said Peg.

"Or someone came and got it," Anna said.

"Are we going to stay here?" Raymer asked.

I shook my head.

"We need to find someplace better to wait," I said. "This is good for an hour. Maybe two. If we see them do something. But we're going to need water. Supplies."

Bem cracked open the bathroom door to a half bath under the stairs. She lifted the lid to the back of the toilet.

"Got some," she said in triumph.

Not to be outdone, Karen took the stairs two at a time and checked the two bathrooms upstairs.

"Same here," she called down.

"Three gallons?" said Brian. "It can last for a little while."

Julie and Peg went to help the girls drain the backs of the tanks into bottles.

"Did you check the garage?" I asked.

"No time," said Brian.

I reached for the knob then thought a second. The house was empty, but my rule was check first. Be prepared.

So I knocked.

There were no moans that answered, no scratches on the other side. Just silence.

I pulled open the door and gasped.

A canary yellow convertible was backed into the far stall, facing out. The one close to us was empty.

The walls of the garage were covered in beach toys. Umbrellas. Chairs. Nets, and seashells. Plastic buckets.

Bikes hung from hooks on the ceiling, dusty beach cruisers for sunshine days.

I stared at the car.

"I don't like that look," said Brian.

"I've got an idea," I told them.

"That's why I don't like it."

5

CHAPTER FIVE

The idea was to get in and get food and get out. Fast.

And it meant splitting up. Against an unknown force.

"This thing could go sideways six ways to Sunday," said Brian as I buckled my seatbelt and rested a rifle on the passenger seat within easy reach.

I leaned up and pressed the button. We both watched the drop top fold up and back and disappear into a little boot at the back of the car.

"I always wanted one of these," Brian sighed.

"I'll let you drive next time."

He harrumphed.

"I'll draw them off," I reminded him. "Lots of noise. Lots of bang bang. You stick with them."

He waved me down.

"I know the plan."

"Stick with it. We're back here in an hour."

"What if we don't find anything?"

I shrugged.

"Then maybe I'll find out where our welcome wagon party is calling home and we go calling on them."

He shivered. I guess I didn't keep the "I'm kidding" look on my face long enough.

"We'll find something," he assured me.

I nodded.

"Drop the garage as soon as I'm clear. Keep everyone together."

"You're counting on me," he finished for me. "We got this."

I gripped the wheel and started the engine.

Brian pressed the garage door opener. Nothing happened and he laughed.

"Power?" he said.

He moved over to the front of the garage door, twisted the handle and lifted it up.

Sunlight flooded into the garage and I jammed the convertible in gear, raced down the short driveway and squealed into the road.

I glanced over my shoulder and saw the door coming down.

Part one done.

Part two. Distraction.

I hit the horn, ducked low in case anyone decided to start shooting and roared down the street. I slammed the gear into second, slid into a wide turn on the corner and the engine screamed as I headed toward the highway.

The highway in this case was the main strip that ran from the causeway all the way to the national park at the end of the island. Six miles long, four lanes wide and not a soul on it.

Except mine.

Wide enough to hold the road, some strip malls and a couple of narrow blocks of houses on either side.

Anyone there would hear me.

I cranked the CD player, just in case, and Bon Jovi provided the soundtrack to the ride.

Distraction was my go to technique for fighting or stealing or just plain surviving. People go for the distraction like a fish for something shiny in the water because that's how we're hard wired.

Danger? Watch for movement.

Hungry? Watch for movement.

Scared? Watch for movement.

Loud fast noises draw our attention and we focus on it with tunnel vision.

It took four minutes to reach the end of the strip and turn around. I'd have to slow down.

I curled into a modified K turn and popped the clutch through the gears back up to speed. Fifty was too slow, eighty too fast for the narrow strip of asphalt.

Hundreds of condos in block developments had empty black windows that could house anyone. Anything.

I didn't think there would be supplies there. Most were rentals, condo-tels leased out by owners to one week vacationers.

If she was hiding on the island, she might hole up in one though.

Bis. Her message led us here.

I don't know how long ago she spray painted the words on a plywood sign outside the refugee camp where she was supposed to be.

But it was there.

Against the odds. The universe loved me, I mused. It must, because I had more luck than a leprechaun.

Until it ran out.

Two tan army transport trucks trundled out of a side road and blocked the way.

Two more belched black smoke from thick pipes as they blocked the road behind me when I passed.

I stopped halfway between them.

Guess my distraction worked.

6

CHAPTER SIX

I was reminded of a line from a poem. Instead of cannons to the left and right of me, there were guns. Enough barrels to make a porcupine blush.

"Turn it off!" one of the men screamed. "Kill the engine."

I listened to the rumble of the motor. It was good advice.

Straight ahead was a house. Stucco over concrete bricks. A scene from a movie flashed through my mind.

The front end of the car smashing through the wall. Debris flying. Airbags popped. Blood.

Then the bullets.

I flicked my eyes up to the rearview mirror. Same house style behind me.

One difference.

The garage.

A carport conversion. Siding instead of brick.

"Get out!" the men started advancing up the road.

Time to do the thing or get off the pot.

I dropped my hand to the gear shift, popped into reverse and shoved the pedal to the metal.

A plume of smoke shot across the yellow hood. The front end shimmied as I rocketed across the yard and half the driveway. Backwards.

I aimed for the garage door.

Prayed it was empty. I think I heard bullets.

The rat a tat followed me for two seconds until the trunk crunched through the thin pressed metal of the door.

A chunk of something whacked me across the back of the head.

The car plowed through the garage and luck was with me. It smashed into the rear wall and everything went gray.

I was lucky.

Sometimes things happen so fast, move so quickly that it's only in the memory of it that you know what happened.

The airbag deployed. A piece of technology designed to save lives in front end collisions still worked just fine when the driver chose to smash through a wall.

There was a bang and a pop, a smash and shatter, the crunch of plastic and crumpled metal and the tick tick tick of fluid as it sprayed on the hot engine and enveloped the garage in boiling steam.

Lucky.

I took a shot to the face and side of the head. Stayed half awake enough to grab the rifle as I folded out of the car and bent toward the door.

Bullets ripped through the fog enshrouded opening and nicked the rifle out of my hand.

I let it go, stumbled over the two steps and fell into a laundry room and kicked the door closed. Another layer between me and the boys with the bullets.

The house smelled like rancid meat. There was a Z in here.

I shoved off the floor and scrambled through the kitchen. The open floor plan put a bar between the living room and sink on the counter.

It wasn't a Z giving off that smell.

A rotting body lay on the couch, the top of her head missing. The only way I could tell it was a woman was the dress.

A man sat across from her, shotgun at his feet, half his head gone as well. A pact for the end of the world.

I tried not to gag as I reached for the gun. Checked the rounds. Two gone, four more for the pumping.

I jacked a new round in the chamber and aimed at the front door as I backed toward the slider.

My foot slipped in sticky goo and I fell over on my ass.

As the front door shredded. Bullet tore through the hollow metal panels and buzzed over my head, angry hornets of death.

I scooted, aimed from my back and waited.

They kicked in the front door and two rushed in as it bounced back on them. The door hit number two and shoved him slightly sideways.

The shotgun went off like a cannon in the enclosed space and pounded a slug into each of them.

It made the others hesitate.

Just enough for me to hit the slider and fight it open. It was stuck. Wouldn't budge.

I slammed the butt of the shotgun into the glass, ducked as it sparkled in shards around me and crawled out as the second wave of bandits screwed up their courage and came in shooting.

The back yard was shallow, narrow, surrounded by a fence. Two shots against how many men and how many bullets, I wasn't sure.

No way to know.

I ran for the fence as fast as I could, expecting shots from the side of the house. But whoever was in charge of this boondoggle didn't flank the house.

Just sent the men through the front.

I hit the fence, jumped, hopped and plopped on the other side.

The gray spots from the crash came back and blossomed black, like an eclipse on the Florida sun.

I could hear the men pounding through the back door on the other side, boots slapping the concrete of the patio.

I rolled over and crawled, scrambled in the dry brown grass and sand.

A dead dog's body was chained to a red doghouse. I curled up on the far side of the doghouse and waited.

I could see the shadow of the fence and a round head pop over it, the voice shouting.

"Clear!"

Then it moved on. I held still. Trying to breath. Trying not to pass out.

I lost that fight.

$$7$$

CHAPTER SEVEN

I woke up later.

How much later, I wasn't sure. Hours, maybe.

Long enough that it would matter. People might come looking for me. My people.

And I didn't want them out there for the bandits to find.

Another thing about a car crash that no one talks about is the ache. It hurts.

The trauma makes every muscle sore and add to it other injuries from dumb moves in my cross country romp and I'm sad to say it took a few moments to get up and limber.

Before the Z, I would schedule a massage and imagine a happy ending while they worked on the knots, and pounded out the pain.

Now I couldn't imagine such a luxury.

I listened before I moved too much. It was quiet enough to stand, stretch, wait for the blood to restore feeling.

The body of the dog and almost melted into the earth and I sent a curse after the people who just left it chained up to die. Maybe they met a similar fate.

They did.

The sliding glass door opened to my pull, released a noxious cloud of dead fumes, two bodies laid out on the floor, tiny holes in the back of their heads, shot execution style.

Maybe they didn't mean to kill their dog, I thought as I looked at the cabinets. Empty, doors open.

Someone took everything.

The bandits, I suspected. Killed these people. Took their food. Didn't free their dog.

I let a surge of hate gurgle in my gut. Kids and dogs. Anyone who would hurt either had a special place in hell and I wanted to help them get there.

But I had to get to my people first.

The road in front of the house was empty. The two transport trucks gone.

I could see the twin skid marks of burned rubber leading across the asphalt to the house next door, but that was the only damage visible from this angle.

The front door unlocked with a click and I opened it to a gust of salty tinged wind slipping in from the ocean side of the island as I stepped out onto the porch.

The cold steel of a barrel poked against the side of my head and bounced.

"Got you," a young thin reedy voice said.

I slowly lifted my hands in surrender, glanced out of the side of my eyes.

It was a kid, little more than at least. Byron's age. All elbows and knock knees and a bad case of acne that dotted his cheeks like blush.

"Don't move," he warned and took a deep breath.

He was going to shout for help. Scream maybe.

The glance showed me his finger wasn't on the trigger. Me walking out of the door must have surprised him as much as he surprised me.

I kept my hands moving up and whipped them up and twisted. The move knocked his gun up, toward the house, and I had enough time to glimpse his wide eyes before I jammed the heel of may palm into his nose.

Blood splotched across the sand drizzled porch as he plopped over backwards, yanked the rifle with him as he fell and hauled on the strap.

The hit was enough to blast starbursts in his eyes, but the kid was tough. I had to give that to him.

He crab crawled backwards, mouth working through a sheet of blood that fountained from his misshapen nose, fingers discovering how to reach the trigger, how to aim.

I planted one foot on the porch and the other between his spread legs before he could get too far.

He forgot about the gun, forgot his name even as both hands cupped his smashed groin. He opened his mouth to howl. I dropped down and punched him in the stomach.

His diaphragm spasmed as he struggled to breath, the two hits curling him over on his side, so painful he couldn't even moan. That kind of hurt is intense agony, the only relief is in freezing and remaining still.

Still and silent.

I looked around.

There was a guy at the house on the other side of the car crash, waiting by the door. His back to us as he leaned against the rail, waiting.

They left two to stand watch, maybe more that I couldn't see. I was too exposed out here, to vulnerable.

What I needed was more information.

I grabbed my guard by the ankle and hauled him through the front door, into the house and clicked it closed behind us.

8

CHAPTER EIGHT

There is something to be said for the resiliency of youth. I'd been kicked in the nuts before not too long ago and it felt like it took me a lot longer to recover than the kid.

By the time I had him in a chair and used shoelaces from the two dead bodies to tie him up, he was breathing and glaring.

But he hadn't started talking yet. Or screaming, so maybe he wasn't recovering as fast as I thought.

He just showed it better than I did.

"Are you going to shoot me?" he grunted.

"Too loud," I told him.

He seemed to consider this and nodded.

"You want me to talk," he said.

He knew. Smart kid. He didn't need me to tell him. He squared his jaw anyway.

"I'm not telling you shit."

I stared at him. Let the silence stretch for a few moments until it got uncomfortable. Most people can't stand the quiet. Nature abhors a vacuum and human nature wants to fill it with noise.

Before the Z, it was radios and television, mindless chatter. We called it small talk because it signified nothing. Small talk from scared minds afraid of what might happen in the void.

Silence is boring, the Boy had told me once when he heard I drove sixteen hours from Florida with the radio off. Nothing but the hum of the tires on the road and the wind against the windshield in my ears, and the thoughts that bubbled up in silence such as that.

I told him that the only way to hear something was to listen. I tried to make it sound deep and meaningful, wise words from his old man he could repeat to his own children one day.

But I think he thought me a fool.

Why listen to the quiet when there is such a thing as a guitar solo.

Still, my ability to just be served me well in the long runs, and long drives and served me still even now as the pimple faced boy stared up at me and began to babble.

Just to fill the void.

I was glad he decided to talk instead of scream, but his rifle in my hands may have helped him make that choice. No need to threaten someone who can conjure up worse things in their mind.

His name was Jamie and he was nineteen, though folks thought he looked younger. He worked at a gas station before the Z, and he was part of a group of hard chargers and bad asses that owned the island now.

They were going to kill me and my friends for trespassing, and take all of our stuff.

I didn't bother to correct him that we had no stuff, and in fact, were looking to get supplies on this side of the island, just to tide us over in a house to house hunt for clues or answers.

The sign that led us here didn't exactly put an X on the spot we needed to find.

Jamie kept talking. His family was gone, the group the only people he had left. He was from south of Daytona, and it was lost to the Z, just like Orlando and the rest of Florida. Probably.

I didn't ask questions. Just kept watching him. I watched him talk, shift, twitch and squirm as he filled the silence with information.

But it wasn't good information.

I didn't care about his name, or his history. I wanted to know how many men were still hunting out there. What their resources were. And most importantly, how to avoid them while I did a hunt of my own.

His eyes flicked over my shoulder and I ducked to one side as the front door popped in and two bodies slammed through shooting.

They shot Jamie. They shot the spot where I had been standing. The slider shattered as a third bandit crashed through in a hail of bullets and shards of glass.

A firefight is chaos. Smoke fills the air, the acrid scent of powder assaults the sinuses. Explosions and noise rip at the eardrums, and death is imminent. A second and a centimeter away.

The person who can survive a firefight is the one who can keep their head when all about them are losing theirs.

I kept my head low. Covered with my forearms and elbows while I cowered on the floor next to the island bar that separated the living space from the kitchen.

Bullets ripped through walls. Pounded through glass and chipped the counter, spraying the floor with sharp splinters of wood and tile.

Jamie pitched over backwards, blood leaking from holes in his chest and stomach.

His wide gray eyes stared at me as he died.

Then the bullets stopped. The bodies of the men who made the assault stood up, surveyed the scene.

I assumed their eyes were drawn to the dead kid on the floor. His blood pooling in a widening circle of crimson.

They could tell he was dead. They may have assumed the same about me, my back against the shattered wood, curled up on the floor too.

I don't know if they relaxed. Or if they were in shock at killing one of their own.

It didn't matter.

I flinched the rifle around, aimed center mass at the biggest one and pulled the trigger. Pulled it again at the second guy next to him at the front door.

Twirled it on the third guy. Too late.

He grinned at me over the barrel of his gun aimed at my face.

The top of his head erupted in a geyser of goo that splatted onto the tile floor. He crumpled on top of it.

Tyler's boots crunched in the glass as he stepped through, gun at the ready. Byron and the Boy followed.

"Are you hit?" Tyler asked as he stood over me.

"Not my blood," I said.

He reached down and helped me up. I held on to the bar for a moment as the blood pounded in my head.

Byron moved past and scooped up weapons and ammunition. He tossed a couple of magazines to the Boy who slid them into pockets.

"We kicked over the beehive, Dad."

"You were supposed to stay with the others," I said.

I was talking to him, but it was meant for them all.

"You're welcome," said Bryon.

He toed the corpse of the guy who would have shot me as he stepped past it.

"There are more out there," said Tyler. "We need to get moving."

I took a breath, held it for a four count, then let it out slow for another four count. Then did it again.

They were right. We needed to move.

I checked Jaimie's rifle for ammunition and motioned to Tyler to lead the way.

9

CHAPTER NINE

They led me through the back door and across the yard to the fence at the rear.

Tyler stood guard while Byron hopped over. The Boy followed, then I pulled myself up and managed not to fall on the other side. Tyler landed gracefully next to me.

Youth is wasted on the young.

We crept on the edge of the fence down an alleyway that separated the houses on this block.

The grid spit us out on a feeder road that led to the river in one direction and the ocean in the other.

We could hear the ocean surf pounding the shore, a relentless reminder that despite all we were going through, mother nature stayed the same.

Tyler motioned Byron forward and took rear point. They kept the Boy and I in the middle. I almost didn't let them.

Danger was still out there, still hunting, and it could strike at any moment.

But I wanted to be near my son, to protect him if things went bad.

They didn't.

Byron pushed open a wrought iron gate and latched it closed when the other three were all through.

It was a mini-mansion on the beach, a Mediterranean style construction that looked indestructible. Marble columns bracketed the solid oak door that opened as we approached.

Bem and Anna stood aside to let us pass and closed the door behind us with a solid thunk.

"At least you hide in style," I said.

Anna shook her head.

Bem was more diplomatic.

"You look like crap, Dad."

"Who me?"

"I didn't want to say anything," said the Boy.

I let Anna direct me into the giant living room that overlooked a wall of glass facing the beachfront. A pool full of green water marred the view, but the blue ocean beyond looked serene.

Brian and the others huddled around a small smokeless fire in the marble fireplace.

"You like?" he said as he moved to help Anna.

There was no need to clean off the pristine granite counters. She laid out rags and medical supplies, what few there were and went to work on the cuts and scrapes.

The bruising and swelling would go away on their own. Given time.

I wasn't sure how much of that we had.

"We found a boat," said Brian. "It can ferry us back in the morning."

"This place has been picked clean," Peg said from her spot next to the fireplace.

"I'm not leaving yet," I groaned as Anna wiped a particularly deep gash I didn't know I had.

"We found a note Dad," Bem said. "It's from her."

"I want to see it."

"We don't think you should go back out there," said Anna.

"It was hers," said the Boy. "She said she's going home."

Home. Crap.

Home was Oviedo, a small community just north of Orlando. Thoughts of the sea of cars we blew up on our way out flickered in my mind.

There were five million people in Central Florida. Five million more on the Tampa side of the peninsula, and a couple of million more on the coast where we were.

"That's a hell of a lot of Z," I sighed.

"She's smart," said Bem. "She'll leave another note for us to find her."

I nodded, more to flinch away from the sting than agreeing.

"Tell me," I said.

"Dad, I'm going home. Bis," said the Boy.

"That's it?"

"That's it."

"Where?"

"Her house, I think," he answered.

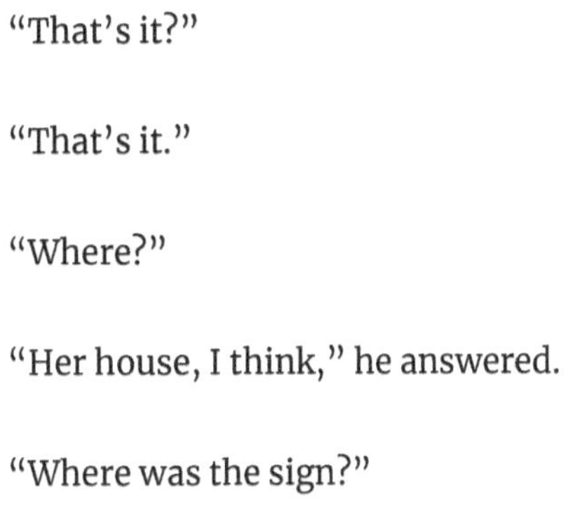

"Where was the sign?"

"Gnarly Surf Shack."

This time the nod was real. It was a breakfast spot we went to every visit to the beach. Get to the sand early to find a spot to park and walk up the main strip to a little outdoor café on the river next to the drawbridge.

She loved it. We loved it.

"Boat?" I turned to Brian.

"We get back to the bus and go get her," he said with an enthusiasm I didn't feel.

He hadn't been in a car crash and a firefight, so he could feel that way.

I looked past them to the window. Long shadows stretched across the sand as the sun dipped toward the Gulf on the other side of the state.

She was an hour away.

One hour.

Twenty minutes in the boat. Twenty minutes back to the bus. Ten minutes to get to the river from where we were.

Two hours to her house.

A trip that had taken far too long brought me right back to where I started. Where I hid and lost my kids the first time.

"Let's get moving," I said.

"We think we should go in the morning," said Brian.

He bit his lip and glanced over his shoulder for support from the others. They nodded their heads.

"We can camp in the bus if we lose daylight," I said.

"It's not just that," Peg said. "We're tired. You're tired. We've been going hard for weeks."

She was right.

But we were only two hours from her. I said as much.

"But if she's not there when we arrive," said Brian. "If there's another note that sends us someplace else, we'll be spending the night in Z central."

He motioned to the mansion.

"We have a good spot for the night. We can leave at dawn."

"There are men out there hunting us," I reminded him.

"They don't know we're here," said Tyler.

"You need to rest," Bem said.

The Boy nodded. I could see the others too. All nodding. All agreeing with each other.

I stood up and wobbled. Not much. But the blow to my head may have had something to do with it.

Anna put her hand on top of mine and I realized I was holding the edge of the counter for balance.

"Okay," I said.

They watched me, but no one said anything. Guess my wobble made them wonder. Made them worry.

Made me worry too. The world wasn't tilting sideways yet, and vertigo hadn't started a doppler tunnel effect.

Still, I could use some rest. Maybe not sleep, because I think the rule is concussions shouldn't go to sleep. But rest and food would be good.

"Food?"

There was much shaking of sad heads around me.

"Everywhere we look is empty," said Brian.

The hunters, whoever they were, had scavenged the entire island. I almost made the argument that we should take the boat and fish along the way, but kept my mouth shut instead.

We would go to bed without supper that night. It wouldn't be the first time.

10

CHAPTER TEN

I sat up in the dark and glared at the room around me.

There were mattresses and comforters spread on the tile floor around the fireplace, sleeping bodies curled or splayed on them.

I studied the darkness for what disturbed me.

Raymer snored. Lou whimpered, some dream making her foot twitch.

Anna lay still next to me, the Boy on one side of her, Bem and Tyler on the other. Close enough that it made me want to growl.

But it wasn't in the house.

Something outside, some noise or shadow flitting across the glowing cat smile of the crescent moon making the sand glow two shades brighter than the dark water.

I pushed to the edge of the mattress and stood, picked my way across the cold tile to the floor to ceiling windows that made up the rear wall.

I made an argument for sleeping upstairs, but this room was big enough for all of us. There was safety in numbers, even if the glass made me feel exposed.

The darkness beyond stretched unbroken to the north and south, curving with the shoreline.

Once, before the Z, I had gone out in a boat after dark and the Florida coast looked like Christmas lights in the night. There were dark places along the way, natural conservation areas, especially around Cape Canaveral and the Space Center.

But here, where we were, there was a long line of condos and developments that stretched as far north as St. Augustine. A couple of thousand buildings facing the water.

A few hundred more to the south.

All dark. All empty.

A shadow moved across the sand. A body. Too quick to be a Z. Trying to sneak.

We hadn't made it back to the mansion unseen. Or maybe our feeble fire stood out like a lighthouse through the glass windows, and we were just too cocky, too naïve to notice.

Someone did though, and my money was on the hunters.

They found us, and they were moving in.

I opened my mouth to say something. To wake the others and get everyone moving.

But to where?

A mad dash for the boat in the dark?

How many would we lose that way? How safe would that be?

Would we be running into a trap? An ambush set up and waiting for the bodies on the beach to flush us out?

I shook my head and ignored the ache at the base of my skull. The gash there probably needed stitches and I was a good candidate for a concussion, but there was no time for pain.

The thing about running long distances was learning to compartmentalize and ignore the aches. They were there, but they couldn't stop you.

I turned back to the room and found the Boy standing by the fireplace.

He picked his way over to me.

"You saw something," he mouthed into my ear.

I nodded.

"Do you want my help?"

I nodded again.

"Stay here. No one goes out," I whispered into his ear.

"I can back you," he answered.

"This is backing me. Keep them safe. Keep them quiet if they wake."

I leaned back, but a shadow fell across his face and I couldn't see his reaction. I wasn't sure if he could see mine either. The moon was bright outside, but in here, all it offered was shapes and insinuations.

The Boy reached for my hand and put it on top of his head. I curled my fingers into his hair and he nodded, letting me know he was following my play.

I patted his face with my palm, then trailed my finger along the wall to the stairs and climbed them.

It was darker upstairs.

The long tall windows below let in meager light from the moon, but up there, the doors to the rooms were closed.

I played the part of a blind man feeling my way to a door, twisted the knob and slipped into one of the bedrooms we had taken a mattress from.

I moved slow toward the window and wondered if I could be seen from the beach as I reached through the curtain and slid up the double paned glass.

It looked over a faux balcony, a narrow one foot space with a balustrade that led to the true balcony off the master bedroom. The design was for effect, but it would have been smarter for me to go back in and exit through the master.

As it was, I slid over the sill of the window and edged to the true balcony. I slipped over the side, made my way to the corner and shimmied down the slick column.

Slipped on the salt crushed thin marble. My boots made too much noise as I landed, and I crouched in the shadow of the column, waiting to see if I had been heard.

There were four shadows moving across the beach, two from either direction.

Closer now. They slipped up the shallow dune and climbed onto the walkway, skipping the gate.

Guess they didn't want to chance a squeak.

Four on one. I hated those odds, but I had surprise on my side.

They hit the wide pool deck and split up again. Two moving on the pavers toward where I was hiding, the other two on the far side of the patio.

Far enough in the dark that it was difficult to make out details on them.

I hoped that would work to my advantage, and wished I had woken Tyler and Byron as additional back up.

The time for wishing was over.

The two shadows evolved into men, gun toting hunters with eyes locked on the glass. Watching for movement. Checking to make sure they weren't discovered.

The first one passed the column I was behind and I held my breath. The second followed and two steps past me, I reached out, grabbed his chin and lifted. I made a swipe with my other hand and cursed as blood squirted out of his neck and made a wet, slopping sound on the tile pavers.

The first one turned, enough time to open his mouth and make a gurgle before I jammed the point of the knife home in his Adam's apple.

He dropped the gun and it clattered on the bricks.

The other two opened up, muzzle flashes crackling in the dark.

I dropped to the deck and rolled for the column.

Bullets chewed up the brick pavers, razor sharp chips slicing through the skin on my arm and face.

Two single shots rang out and the hail of fire stopped.

I glanced up and could see the shadow of the Boy in the door behind two mounds on the deck.

He stepped aside and Byron moved past him to strip the fallen of their weapons and ammunition.

"There'll be more," he called out.

There were.

Bullets sailed over his head and crashed the windows, showering the group inside in a rain of crystalized glass.

More shadows on the beach, just a couple of bodies shooting as they ran toward the boardwalk from the house to the sand.

The gate squeaked open as Byron crawled toward the door. I didn't see the Boy and panic clenched my gut. Had he been hit?

No time to check. I grabbed the rifle from number two, sliced the strap that trapped it under the dead weight of his body and aimed at the end of the wooden sidewalk where it touched the deck.

The shadows kept firing as they ran, reached the brick pavers and I opened up in quick bursts.

They pitched forward, sideways and one slid across the deck and dropped into the pool.

Then the men up front opened fire.

11

CHAPTER ELEVEN

There is no alarm clock quite like a machine gun redecorating the walls of the house you happen to be hiding inside.

The builders of the home weren't cheap. They used real marble and thick brick under the stucco walls, so the bullets only sounded like thunder slapping the sides of the house.

The windows were another story.

When the four now dead men tried to make their beach run toward us and took out the wall of windows, they woke everyone up in a hail of clattering glass.

The front door and windows facing the street shattered under the new assault.

"Keep low!" I heard Brian scream and people crawled out of the house and onto the pool deck.

My people.

"Beach!" I pointed and The Boy nodded from the ground where he cowered.

I watched him whisper into the ears of people as they crawled past him, and then nodded as they shimmied around the pool and moved toward the wooden boardwalk.

I strapped the stolen rifle to my back and shimmied up the marble column to the balcony.

I wish I could say it took no time. That it was easy. That my monkey like dexterity combined with athletic prowess made the climb almost super heroic easy.

And if I lived to retell it, and no one who was watching contradicted me, that would be my story.

But in reality, there was grunting. And groaning. Some moaning. My forearms burned as I wrapped them around the marble. My feet cramped as I gripped with all I had.

Everyone made it to the sand before I made it to the balcony.

I wanted to scream to them to hide in the dunes, but I was too busy trying to catch my breath.

Brian or Byron directed them there anyway.

Then whoever was shooting out front came in through the front door and lit up the inside of the mansion.

I stumbled across the upper balcony and this time used the master bedroom door.

The inside landing was still dark, except for the yellow muzzle flashes of automatic weapons blinking like lightning from the room below.
   I laid down, aimed through the rails and sighted on a group of shadows that congregated inside the door.

None of them survived.

There were others though, inside the main living room, and outside the front door.

They zeroed in on my shots and tried to remove my hiding spot.

But I wasn't there. I moved further back in the darkness.

Something small, round and sounded like a baseball thudded onto the carpet five feet away.

I sprinted through the bedroom, made the door to the balcony when the world blew up around me.

Lifted me up, sent me over the rail. So fast I didn't have time to windmill. To scream.

Just a quick vision of the black smooth deck rushing up to meet my face.

Then muck.

Stinking green muck and a belly flop into the rancid waters of the pool.

I crashed into the dead guy floating in the water and floundered up, let go of the rifle that was trying to drag me down.

Bounced my forehead off the edge of the pool. Crawled out and scraped toward the boardwalk.

A hand reached over the side of the wood and yanked me into the dunes, then dragged me into the shadows under the walkway.

Someone put a finger on my lips, but they need not have bothered. The edge of the board clipped my rib as they pulled and I didn't have enough air to breath, let alone scream.

Bootsteps pounded above us. Sand rained down through the cracks in the board.

"Where are they?" a gravelly voice rasped. "Keep searching."

I could have shot him. If I had a gun. Mine was at the bottom of the swimming pool.

I reached for Brian's and he pushed my hand away. I dug for my knife instead, but someone else pinned that hand to my side.

Hot breath breezed into my ear as Anna leaned her head into mine. Willing me to be still. Willing me to be quiet.

I listened to what they weren't saying and kept still.

12

CHAPTER TWELVE

We could see them searching the beach as dawn broke over the ocean. The horizon slipped from black to purple to the gray light of morning just before the sun peeked up.

They were looking for tracks, and when they didn't find them, I wasn't sure what they would do.

We hid in the darkness under the boardwalk as a dozen tromped out to the sand, and back again. Crunching on the shattered glass.

There would be enough light soon to follow the water trail I left from the pool to the edge of the walkway.

That might be enough to make them look.

Whoever was directing the search didn't make the men fan out. He sent them south, searching from shore to the edge of the dune.

I grabbed Brian by the shirt and pulled his ear close to my mouth.

"Go," I breathed and pointed north. "Stay inside the dune."

He nodded.

There was a shallow depression between the dunes and the million dollar homes that lined the sea front.

I hoped we could make it a few houses up or more, then cut inside to the road and run for the river where the promised boat waited.

Brian tapped Peg, who in turn tapped Anna.

They began crawling, each tapping the next in line.

I grabbed Tyler's rifle before he took off after Bem and held it. He glanced at me, then reached into the waist of his pants and pulled out a pistol before he followed her.

One by one they crawled away as I watched the boardwalk above and the men out by the dune.

The light grew brighter. Still no sun, but it was moments away, and when it was up, the cloudless sky would shine a spotlight where we were and where we went.

Byron and the Boy stopped five houses away, far enough and dim enough I couldn't make out their features, just the shape of them as they turned and waited.

Their turn to watch over me.

My body screamed as I began crawling. Wet clothes covered in sand, aching muscles stiff and swollen. No telling what kind of bacteria from the pool in the scrapes and wounds.

I moved fast, as fast as I could toward them.

Byron lifted his rifle and sighted over me, and I froze, but the Boy waved me forward.

I glanced back just to be sure.

There was no one there, no one watching, but the hunters had turned and they were making their way back to the mansion.

The light was bright enough they would see our passage in the sand.

I popped up to hands and knees and crawled faster.

Brian picked a good exit point between two houses. The yellow grass didn't show prints, but I could see the churned sand that marked our way like a beacon.

I stopped at the Boy and Byron.

"Do you know where the boat is?"

"I do," the Boy stammered before Byron could say anything.

"Get them there," I told Byron and pushed him toward Brian and the rest of them.

"Make a mess," I said to the Boy and pointed further up the dune.

He turned and began crawling, swirling sand in his passage, churning up more track for the hunters to trace. I followed in his wake, adding my own trail to his.

Six houses further, I grabbed his ankle and didn't mention the yelp he let escape from his lips.

He turned inland and scrambled on the shell pathway until we were hidden from the beach by trees and homes. Then we stood.

"Take us to the river," I said. "Eyes up."

I wasn't sure if there were more hunters on this side, or searching for us.

But we needed to be careful.

13

CHAPTER THIRTEEN

We made the boat without encountering any hunters. Tyler, Bem and Brian stood on the shore, waiting.

It was a thirty two foot party barge on triple pontoons, and I was glad to see Brian had outfitted everyone with an oar.

We were going to run silent across the water.

No one said a word as the Boy traded his gun for a paddle and sat near his sister at the front of the pontoon.

Brian directed me to the seat behind the wheel, spun it around to face the stern.

"Keep watch," he said.

He shoved us off from the pier, and let the slow current catch us. We didn't so much as paddle as meander. He let the river do the work, pulling us downstream toward the North causeway and the mouth of the river where it met the ocean.

He sat on the back of the boat and used a paddle as a rudder.

I'd have to ask him where he learned the skill, and it was a skill. He steered into the current and zig zagged across the river.

I wanted to watch, maybe to pick something up, but I kept my eyes trained on the bank we left behind.

"Now," Brian called as we reached the halfway mark and the others began paddling.

At first, their rhythm was off, but after a few strokes they settled into a steady pull together.

I had guessed twenty minutes to cross the river the night before. I was off by five. We made it in fifteen.

Brian steered us toward a common dock at a park, less than ten minutes from where we parked the bus.

A ping bounced off the roof of the pontoon and I saw the flash of sunlight on a lens on the other side of the river.

Figures gestured and pointed back where we were, two hundred yards or so away.

One of them aimed a rifle at us and fired again.

We couldn't hear the echo of the gunshot. It was caught by the wind and carried away from us, too far to travel across the water.

But the bullet clanked into the console next to me.

I lifted the rifle and aimed back. Aimed high for wind, to the right for the drop and shot.

It slammed into the guy next to the shooter and pitched him sideways into the water.

I was aiming for the shooter.

We bounced off the wood dock and Brian leaped up. He wrapped a thin rope around a post and started shoving people up and over.

We were too exposed out on the water, the dock open to the sky, and the far side of the river.

But there was a building, an event center fifty yards further away.

He directed them toward it, and they ran hunched over, toward the shelter of the structure.

I stood on the stern of the rocking ship and shot back but I didn't hit anyone else.

Blame the waves, the light bouncing off the water, or maybe my fear of someone hitting one of us.

But I kept their aim off. They were just as scared of getting shot.

Brian rolled onto the dock.

"Go! Go!" he shouted and I popped up and pounded after him.

Once we put the building between us and the shooters, I took a breath.

"Anyone hit?" I asked.

"You are," said the Boy.

I looked down. There was a hole in my shirt, hole in my stomach.

"Shit," I said.

"They're coming," Byron called out as he peered around the wall of the building. "They've got a boat too."

Anna lifted my shirt and tried to examine the wound.

"We've got to move," I said.

Or think I did. It may have come out a little warbled. Garbled.

"We've got to move," Brian shoved Raymer and Peg toward the bus.

Tyler grabbed me by one arm, the Boy the other and helped me stumble toward after the group as we ran.

Anna ripped my shirt as we pounded along. I had it easy. The two boys were almost carrying me.

She tied a strip of cloth around my midsection, cinched it tight.

"Ow," I groaned.

"Oh that you feel," she snapped.

The bus hove into view. Still there. Untouched. Waiting.

Peg opened the doors and cranked the engine. Everyone dashed on board in a mad scramble of limbs and grunts.

Or maybe that was me as Tyler and Brian grabbed my arms and helped me in. The Boy lifted my feet.

They laid me down in the back as the rumble of the engine grew louder and Peg did her best imitation of me in a yellow convertible as she burned rubber to get us going.

14

CHAPTER FOURTEEN

I expected chaos. I got Anna and Bem.

They kneeled on either side of me, working in tandem.

"Through and through," Anna said as she tilted me to one side and removed the shirt tied around me.

"We have to stop the bleeding," Bem said.

"It may have nicked something," said Anna. "This is going to hurt."

She warned me.

Then she stuck her finger inside of me. It was just the pinky, just the tip to feel around and I didn't scream.

I closed my eyes, gritted my teeth and when I opened them again, they were done.

Who said there's no dignity in passing out from pain. It let me skip some of the hard stuff.

That's not to say it didn't hurt.

It did. A lot.

The slick mess on the floor, wadded up sheets stained crimson and black, and the tight dressing wrapped around my middle let me know they had done some work.

"Look at me," Anna said, eyes locked on mine. "You're going to get an infection. We need to find medicine. Alcohol."

"Whatever was in the pool was on your skin," Bem said. "It's in you now."

I nodded. I got it. As soon as I moved my head, I got it even more. Fever. Aches.

"How long was I out?"

"Twenty minutes," Brian peeked over the seat to the section we had cleared for sleeping in the back. "Your son knew the way so he's directing Peg."

I tried to sit up, fought a wave of nausea and black cloud in my vision.

"That's a fast infection," I said.

"It may be more," Anna sniffed. "We don't know what was in the water. Or on the bullet."

I nodded. Or tried to.

"We'll find what we need," I said. "A bottle of whiskey will work wonders."

"I like an old fashioned," Brian said.

I reached out for Anna's hand with one of mine. Reached for Bem with the other.

They were nice enough to ignore my grimace.

"You've pulled me through worse," I told Anna.

She shook her head.

"Not like this."

"It's just a flesh wound," I glanced at Brian.

He snorted.

"You're scaring us," he said in a soft voice. "You don't have to take all the chances."

I wanted to tell him it wasn't my idea to get shot. That some idiot with a rifle got lucky.

But I kept quiet.

And hoped my luck hadn't run out. I needed it to hold til we reached Oviedo. Til we found Bis.

Then we could hole up someplace off the grid and I'd heal. With or without whiskey.

"Water," I said. "I need water."

Bem passed me a bottle and I sipped the sulfur tang of Florida's aquifer, tried not to gag.

"We're going to be fine," I told them as I leaned back in the blanket.

My tired body was ready for a rest. I just needed to hold out for forty minutes. An hour tops.

Then we'd find her.

"Rest," Anna tucked a blanket in around me.

A nap until we got there. That sounded good.

15

CHAPTER FIFTEEN

We didn't know it was over until it was. Bullets ripped through the side of the bus, shattering windows that fell in razor sharp bits of shrapnel. People screamed and ducked, fell to the floor, bits and bloody sprays arced across the seats.

Peg slumped out of the driver's seat, one hand gripped on the wheel. It yanked the bus sideways, carried it off the road. The long roaming home of ours for the past few weeks bounced off the asphalt, across slick grass and tilted.

The speed of the bus, the angle of the berm, all worked together and sent it tilting up on two wheels. A crazy stunt if it were a movie, but full of screaming men, women and children it was a rolling nightmare.

Gravity grabbed the roof and completed the tilt, slammed the side of the vehicle into the sandy brown dirt. It slid into a palm tree that crumpled a dent in the roof.

We were bounced around. Off the floor, into the side of the bus that was now the floor. Bodies jammed against cracked and blasted windows.

Screams of fear replaced with wails of terror, and pain and grief. Bullets still pinged off the undercarriage of the bus, but we were safer now, the thick iron acting as a shield.

It bought us time. Moments only, maybe. But time.

I stood up and grabbed the side of a seat above my head for balance. The world was still spinning, salty sticky blood leaking from a cut in my hair, another over that eye. My side burning like a hot poker shoved through it.

My hip hurt where I landed. Stiff, swollen.

"Rifle!" It came out as a croak.

Besides, no one was listening to me.

Weak light leaked through the shattered front windshield, a spiderweb of reflections on the wall of the bus. Now the floor.

Brian crawled, dragging an ankle as he skittered toward Peg. She lay at an awkward angle on the door, blood on her head, her arms, her face.

I took a step forward. My boot hit the rifle I wanted and I bent over to pick it up.

And woke up with a new scuff mark on my face. Barrel under my fingers. I gripped it and scooted to my back.

People still cried, wails and snuffles, so I must have only dropped for a second, maybe two.

Long enough for shadows to appear at the back door. Hands working the exterior handle.

I watched the emergency bar on the inside slip up in a half circle, a crack of light lining the upper edge of the door as the shadows stepped back to let it fall open.

Then the grip was in my hand, the stock against my shoulder as I sat up, let the tunnel vision narrow my field of focus to just the heads that appeared in the light.

Pop. Pop. Pop. Three dropped as they tried to peek in, the rest of the shadows fell back.

A hand grabbed me by the collar and yanked me behind a seat as they fired back. Bullets bit into the metal, sliced into the seats, puffed out bits of stuffing, but the layers kept most of us safe.

For a moment.

Byron grabbed Tyler and the Boy. Kicked out the shattered windshield and they began shooting before they rolled out.

I saw them split. Two toward the front of the bus. The Boy used the hood to climb to the side that was our roof. He pounded down it.

I could hear them shooting, firing. The chatter of their rifles as they concentrated fire on a position slightly behind us.

Their movement drew the hunters.

I shoved up, lurched to the open emergency door and leaned out. Took my time. Aimed. Fired.

Rat. A. Tat. Tat.

The gunfire stopped. Smoke drifted across the ambush sight. Dead bodies littered the asphalt above where we crashed.

The Boy dropped off the roof. Tyler and Byron limped around the front of the bus. Tyler cradled his left arm, blood cascading down the thin fabric of his shirt.

Hurt. But alive.

I didn't know if I could say that about the rest of us.

16

CHAPTER SIXTEEN

"We were lucky," Brian cursed under his breath.

Damn lucky. I agreed with him. Our wounded were lined up in the shade of palm trees on the side of the road, resting on blankets. Bound. Bloodied. Battered.

But alive.

Even Peg, who was hurt the worst besides me. A slug sliced into the meat of her shoulder, bounced off the bone in the socket and took a nip from her neck as it kept going.

A nicked artery sounded bad, and she was white from blood loss. But alive.

All of us.

I fought back a wave of vertigo, let the world spin for a moment, and then it passed.

"You need to sit," said Anna through swollen lips.

She had landed on her face in the tumble, smacked it against the metal edge of a seat.

Blood clotted in her hair, dried in sprinkles down her shirt.

I could see shadow figures lumber from the woods further back. Our Z friends coming to visit. Coming to check on us to see if we needed help.

Like good neighbors.

"See who can move," I said.

"No one," Brian snapped.

I watched him. Just watched him. He earned the right to snap because he was my best friend after the Z apocalypse. He had saved me. I had saved him.

I was ahead, but who kept count.

"Sorry," he said and trudged to check on our wounded.

I rummaged through the wreckage where Tyler, the Boy and

Byron stacked what we could salvage, and pulled a pike free.

A pike was Brian's invention. Technically, it belonged to the middle ages, a throwback to a sharp bladed spear medieval foot soldiers used to jab, poke and stab their enemies in battle.

Brian just modified it for a new dark ages.

We took long metal fence poles, wrapped the handle in duct tape to make a better grip. Then jammed a machete blade into the far end, wrapped it in wire and tape to make sure it wouldn't come loose in a fight.

Perfect for jabbing. Poking. Stabbing the Z.

Zombies. We called them Z. I think I started it, but it could be something I picked up along the way and just claimed credit for it. Like Brian claiming the five hundred year old pike as his own.

"You need help," the Boy stopped and stared over my shoulder at the eight lumbering dead as they lurched toward our wreck.

"Finish up," I said. "Pack all we can carry."

I hefted the pike and balanced it in my hand. It was nine feet from tip to butt, and I appreciated the distance. In zombie moves or tv shows, the characters would get close and personal with the Z and stab them with three inch folding knives. Or hatchets.

Why risk the bite? Or splatter?

They also wore tank tops and shorts, then acted surprised when they were bit.

I glanced over my shoulder at my group. Even injured, they were covered neck to boot in layers of clothing.

Z weren't super human. They could bite, and tear and rip. But they had to reach skin first.

And despite what any show might broadcast, clothes are tough to rip through.

Not impossible, but strong enough to buy seconds, and time, especially in a fight, is a commodity that can be exploited.

Time and distance.

I levered the pole and aimed the blade at Z number one, sliced it down with a straight pop through a putrid eyeball and kept moving.

My side screamed. Or maybe it was me. If we had eaten last night, I would have thrown it up.

The Z kept coming.

Then Bem was there, and the Boy.

She shot four. He stabbed three.

In less than a minute, the rest of the Z were just as gone.

It was tough to call them dead, because that's what we said the first time they died.

Now, they were gone.

Forever. Unless there was something about the virus we still didn't understand.

Correction: there was everything about the virus we didn't understand. Like how it started. What happened to the rest of the world. What was going to happen to us.

I rested between my kids, letting them hold me up for just a moment.

Then I stood up. As straight as I could, which wasn't saying much.

They needed me. They all needed me. We were injured. Every one of us battered, bruised, bashed.

I just ignored the pain. The flush on my neck and face. The pounding in my head. Ignored it all, and focused on what to do next.

I wiped the ick off the blade on the rotten shirt of the last Z and turned back toward our crash site.

The boys worked on building packs for us to carry our meager supplies. Brian and Anna worked with the injured to get them up and ready to move.

We would be slow. Weighed down. Ripe for the picking from Z or more bandits.

And back in Florida.

One big freaking circle to find my youngest daughter.

17

CHAPTER SEVENTEEN

"Do you think there are others out there like us?"

We stopped to rest again. This was the forth or fifth time. I couldn't keep count. Hell, I couldn't count to five unless I looked at my fingers.

We were stretched out against a fence that ran alongside the road, the other side cleared pastureland.

I looked at him and tried to wiggle my eyebrows. I don't think it worked as well as I thought. Swollen brow, bruised face and all.

"There's no one out there like you."

That earned a half grin, maybe three quarters though it was

hard to tell from the squinting blurring vision the world offered through puffy eyelids.

"I mean roamers. Vagabonding in the Zombie apocalypse," he said. "We don't have a home. We don't have a safe place to rebuild. We just go."

I tried to shrug. Bits hurt.

"I know, I know," he held up placating hands as if I was going to jump up and argue about it. "We're looking for your daughter. We have a mission and then we'll set up someplace safe. But are there people out there doing what we do?"

"Roaming," I croaked.

"Yeah."

"I bet there are."

Brian sighed and settled his back against the side of the fence.

"I wonder who many people we're losing doing that. As a species, I mean."

I almost told him I didn't care. But that wasn't true.

If I didn't care, I wouldn't have helped him and Peg, Anna, or Byron and Hannah. I wouldn't have helped any of the people we met along the way.

I could have just focused on the objective of getting the job done.

Sometimes caring sucked.

"We have to rebuild sometime," he said. "We can't wander the wasteland, nomadic tribes fighting Z, fighting each other. History showed us what we should do, but this time we get to skip all the bad decisions we made before. We get a do-over."

"Still bad men," I said. Or grunted. Probably grunts of the monosyllabic type.

He understood me though.

"They did a study once," I mused.

"Just once?"

"This one, sure, though in all the world, I bet there are hundreds of studies."

"Were."

"Were hundreds," Brian corrected. "Thousands."

"Can I finish?"

"Probably not, but give it a go," he said.

"It was how fast the flu virus spread, before. They put some oil or fluid on a person's hand, then followed with a black light. It spread to a hundred people just on her way home from work. She would touch, they would touch," I demonstrated. "Pretty soon, it was everywhere."

"You think that's how Captain Z spreads?"

"Captain Z? Is that what you want to go with?"

He shrugged.

"I'm trying it on for size."

I shook my head. Starbursts coalesced at the corner of my vision.

"It should be more menacing," I said. "Captain Z sounds like a breakfast cereal."

"I'll keep trying."

"Do that."

"But the spread?"

"There were two stories going around the compound. Safe havens and a cure."

"Rumors," I said. "From who?"

"From whom?"

"That's what I'm asking you?"

"Do you think that wall was a safe haven?" he brought up the one we had seen north of Georgia outside the refugee camp.

"I don't know if anywhere is safe," I answered true.

He nodded.

We needed to get moving again. Needed to find transportation. Needed to find a safe place to sleep for one more night.

Needed to find her, and then we could sleep for days.

"Nobody move," a voice called out behind us from the other side of the wire fence.

18

CHAPTER EIGHTEEN

I moved. It was a half turn to see who was making the threat.

"Do you want to die?"

That was the question the man asked me on the other end of a hunting rifle.

I crossed half of America and back again to hunt for my kids, and now some ranch owner in the middle of Florida wants to know if I want to die.

Want? What's that?

"I don't," I said.

"That's good," he said with a smile. It didn't touch his eyes, just crinkled the wrinkles around his mouth.

Like he had practiced it a lot to share on a public face, but there was no way in hell he meant it.

"Get up," he didn't offer a hand to help.

I stood up on the edge of the road, put almost everything ounce of will in not groaning, and dusted my hands off on my pants.

"You're covered up good," he said, eyes appraising. "Says something about you."

"I'm an open book," I answered.

That earned a real chuckle.

"That I doubt."

"I'm a simple man. Simple man has simple questions."

"Doubt that more than the first one," the white haired man answered.

His eyes roamed over the rest of us.

"You look like crap," he said.

His face was a map of wrinkles, thin hair brushed back from a broad forehead. He wore pants tucked into working cowboy boots, long sleeves covered up his skin, a long machete on one hip, pistol on the other.

"We've been better," I said.

"What are you doing out here?" the rifle held steady in thick hands.

"Just passing through," I told him.

He nodded up the road.

"More of the dead up there," he said. "A lot more."

"Lot where we came from too."

He took that in and nodded.

"You're bleeding."

I glanced down. Blood soaked through the bandages wrapped around my waist. It brought it to mind and the pain flared up, a white hot poker jabbing me, stealing my breath, making the world wobble.

"I'm not beat the worst," I said.

His eyes rested on Peg, covered in blood. Anna, the same. All of us, scraped, beat up and blood soaked.

"I've got a barn you can sleep in," he said. "You get caught out here after dark and get bit, you might turn into my problem."

He pointed up the road.

"There's a gate in the fence half a mile," he said. "Meet me there."

The tall man started walking on his side of the fence in the direction he indicated.

"What do we do?" Brian asked.

I stared at our group.

"We sleep in the barn," I said.

They had to help the others up. It was all I could do to stay standing on my own.

19

CHAPTER NINETEEN

There are people you meet in life who are transitory. It's easy to tell by the way they impact on your day.

Like the guy in line at the bank who smiles and says hi, or the woman walking her dog who waves as you pass by.

The action done and forgotten, leaving only a good feeling and a memory of kindness.

Then there are the permanent kind of figures, those who make such a dramatic impact that, no matter how short the time they spend with you is, it is easy to recall them years later.

I wasn't sure if we had years in the new Z world left, but the man at the fence was that kind of fellow.

Before, he may have been called larger than life. A giant of a man, six six and in cowboy boots even taller. His former frame may have held four hundred pounds, but the zombie diet took care of those pesky lbs.

It left a lot of skin though. He had the look of a football player gone to seed, without the round belly or layers that normally accompany it. Instead, it was loose skin.

It wasn't too abnormal. He just looked like a big boy going hungry.

If I could have bottled that up, I would have made a fortune before the world collapsed.

"Hey, do you wanna lose fifty pounds? Try the zombie diet. Half starvation, half running for your life. Act now and we'll throw in a bottle of scummy pond water to ease your thirst!"

The info-mercials would have done it for millions after midnight.

"Welcome to the Bar-T," he said as he unlocked the gate and swung it open to let us pass.

His voice matched his frame, like a man used to bellowing orders at cowpokes, crackers and cattle, now gone soft and raspy in this silent new world.

"Howdy," said Brian, trying out his cowboy accent.

"You're lucky," said the ranch man. "I was running the fences on this side of the property today. Otherwise," he left it out there.

I looked at the dirt road that led across a cattle grate, the swinging metal bar fence the only thing to prevent Z or marauders from crossing.

Tyler pointed his hand to the left toward a hillock further back on the property and the ranch man nodded in appreciation.

"You've got a sniper on that hill."

"Good eye," he appraised the boy.

"He's got sunlight glinting off his scope or binoculars," Tyler told him. "I spotted him from the trees. Tell him to pull back into the shadows or someone else might take the shot first."

The ranch man's eyes went wider at this, and he fished a tiny walkie talkie off his belt next to a wood handled six gun revolver.

He issued orders into the speaker and waited, watched Tyler as the boy stared at the sniper's nest.

When the boy nodded, the ranch man hooked the walkie talkie back to his belt and smiled.

"Thanks for not shooting him," he said.

"Thanks for not shooting us," Brian answered back.

The tall man's eyes drifted over us, noting the injured and lame.

"Looks like you met trouble?"

His hazel eyes squinted under the brim of his hat, hand hovering on the belt next to his pistol.

He was a tough looking old bird, a throwback to a lost generation. Wrinkled skin turned leathery under the sun, big hands hooked in a permanent curl brought on by years of abuse or arthritis. Or both.

"We're alive," Brian chirped. "Some more than others."

He said it in a light hearted voice, but there was something in the set of his chin. The tall man nodded, a message passed between them.

Yeah, we may have seen trouble, but we're here, and trouble's not. No need to say it out loud. The rancher got it.

The ranch man's eyes continued to rove over us, appraising, studying.

They stopped on mine and froze. I don't play poker but it was a tell if I've ever seen one.

"Huh," he stated.

"Huh?" I asked.

"You're him?"

I could feel the others turn their eyes toward me, a couple of oh crap looks.

"I guess that depends on which him you're talking about," I shifted to one leg.

"I almost missed it," he said, eyes tracing the rough outline of my face. "A lot more scars, and the bruises don't help."

I racked my brain, trying to decide if I knew him. How I knew him.

Did we run together before? He didn't look much like a runner, but a lot of long distance guys were back of the pack runners. Slow and steady, big bodies moving toward a personal goal to finish a race, instead of racing to the finish.

Or maybe I knew him through work, or a presentation.

I'm good with faces, most of the time. But a couple of explosions and knocks on the noggin may have jarred a few things loose inside the gray matter.

"She's got a picture of you on her dresser," he said. "She said you would come."

And then I couldn't breathe.

20

CHAPTER TWENTY

There are some things I've shared about the Z world. Horrible things I've done. Doubts about my abilities as a father. My failures.

The list is long.

But I won't talk about the reunion.

The rancher said his name was Meroni, and led the stumbling lot of us back toward his ranch.

We followed the crushed shell road over two hills and nestled in a small shallow valley was a two story farmhouse and the promised barn, plus a couple of other buildings.

There were people there. Hanging clothes. Working a garden. Tending cattle.

The house and barn were inside another fence, a second layer that looked added, and sturdy. Another line of defense in case the Z got through.

Meroni slowed his pace to match ours, or maybe that was just the speed of old age.

We made the gate and people started to line up at our approach.

Watching. Waiting.

He bade us enter and we did. One of the men who had been working with a cow, moved past us, nodded and closed the gate.

Meroni took us toward the front porch, and called out her name.

She stepped out of the kitchen and I started crying.

And when she saw me, she flew across the yard at a speed that would make Mercury blush.

She hit me in the chest, wrapped her arms around me and the four of us fell in a sobbing heap on the edge of a shell road in the middle of a Florida farm.

And it's mine.

21

CHAPTER TWENTY ONE

I woke up later.

Turns out, reunions make me faint. Or blood loss and pushing across country, killing Z and anyone who stood in my way.

I woke up in the barn on a cot.

A saline bag nailed to a post by the bed, needle clipped into my arm.

Bem, the Boy and Bis sat on the floor beside me, not talking, just staring.

I tried to sit up, but the Boy pushed me back down.

"They had antibiotics," said Bem.

"You did it," said Bis, eyes wide in wonder. "You said you would, and you did."

"For us too," said the Boy.

My three children, sitting on the floor beside me after a zombie apocalypse.

I tried to say something and couldn't get past the lump in my throat.

"He's probably thirsty," said the Boy.

Bis unscrewed the cap to a water bottle and held it to my lips.

I took two big swallows and let the third swish around in my mouth before taking it down too.

Anna and Tyler stood at the door to the barn, like sentinels standing watch.

"Tell me what happened," I managed to croak.

And so, she did.

"Kai was bit by another kid in the camp, because that's what toddlers do," said Bis, her voice becoming sullen and business like.

There was a rhythm to her speech, like she was telling the story of someone else instead of events she had actually witnessed.

But I knew she witnessed them, lived through them, and it broke my heart.

"Kai got sick, and bit Mom," here her voice caught on a squeak. But she swallowed down a lump and kept going. "Mom got sick and attacked Paul. But he got he out. He got me away."

I nodded. Her stepfather had been in her life since she was three, probably considered him his own daughter. His need to protect her would almost be stronger than mine.

Possibly more, since he was there to do it.

"We got out of the camp, and got away," she said. "We met with some other survivors, a small group. He died saving us. The zombies got him too."

She reached up and wiped a tear from her face and my heart lurched, ached for her. She had seen so much. They all had.

And the little voice inside my head told me it was my fault. I should have been there. Should have found them faster, or never been far away in the first place.

I tried to argue against it, the voices that picked and worried at the edge of my doubts, the ones that spoke the loudest and highlighted every mistake I made.

It was a long list.

I let it roll over me, bathed in the depth of the misfortune my dumb decisions have caused. Then it receded, a wave of regret washing out, and all I was left with was a grip on the rock that was now.

She was here. Bem was here. The Boy was here. And I wasn't going anywhere.

The regret kept washing away, receding and I stayed on the rock of now. Clung to it with a death grip, but deep breathes helped. Now, I focused.

"I'm sorry," I said to her and expected a look full of condemnation and anger.

I got it.

"They're dead," she said. Like it was my fault.

"Our mom too," said Bem.

"And Dustin," the Boy added.

We could have gone around the group in front of a campfire and listed all the lost. Everyone there had lost a loved one, more than one.

Except me.

I was alone before the Z pocalypse started, and the three people I cared most about in the world sat beside me.

I hadn't lost anyone. I waited for the group to realize this, and hate me for it. But no one ever did.

Maybe they were wondering who we would lose next, I suppose.

I vowed we wouldn't lose anyone, then realized just how stupid that prayer was. In this new world, it was a foregone conclusion. Not everyone could make it.

So, I vowed to just try harder so they could.

Brian moved into my field of vision.

"Back from the dead," he joked, then stammered.

"Bad taste," I croaked.

"That's why the Z won't eat me."

He glanced at the cots lined up to the end of the barn.

"They're really helping us here," he said.

"Doctor?"

"Medic," Bis answered for him. "Army. Plus medicine."

"They gave you vet quality stuff," said Bem. "But it works."

I looked at the clean bandage around my mid-section, shifted. Everything still hurt. Everything ached. But it would go away.

"He said you could stay," Bis said. "You'll need to work. We all do. But it's safe here."

"He needs to rest," Anna interrupted.

"No," I said as they started to move away. "I'm fine. I'm good. Just stay."

They settled back to the floor and sat with me until I passed out again.

22

CHAPTER TWENTY TWO

"We hear things," Meroni picked a long green weed, stripped it of the leaves and stuck the juicy end into the corner of his mouth.

"You heard about the wall?"

His eyebrows lifted as he asked the question in that way people have when they're curious and searching.

"We saw it," said Brian. "From a distance."

"So it's real," the old man leaned back on his boot heels and chewed on the end of the stalk in his mouth. "I wondered. People make up a lot of things if they think a good story will get them a meal or a safe place to stay."

"There are a half mile of Z pounding against it," said Brian with a shudder.

The memory of it was terrible. We were a mile away, staring through binoculars and the sounds of the dead carried on the wind. They surged in a relentless tide against the thick stone barrier that stretched as far as we could see to the North, and curved away from us to stretch into the sea.

"Like that everywhere?" Meroni asked.

Brian shrugged.

"We don't know. What we saw, though."

The old man nodded.

"I've caught 'em on the barbed wire round here," he told us. "Four strands on fence post stretches around my whole acerage."

"It holds?" Brian asked.

Meroni shrugged.

"My family has been keeping cattle here for almost a hundred years," he said. "I had big city dreams and got away from it all, but it was here when I retired. That's when the real work began. There's always something that wants inside the fence to get the cattle. Rustlers. Panthers. Wolves at one time, though they were hunted out of Florida. Even a gator every so often. The fence keeps most of 'em out. If they get through, I got the fence around the homestead."

He nodded his head toward the white house with the wrap around porch and the barn beside it. A second pole fence circled it like a barricade.

"We ride the outer fence every other day," Meroni said. "Check for breaks. Shore it up if we need."

I wanted to tell him to shore it all up. String up six more strands of barbed wire until it was a solid wall of flesh ripping wire. Then double it again.

Anything to keep my kids safe now that we were all together again.

But I held my tongue.

"I'll ride with you," I offered.

He nodded thanks, took the weed from his mouth and tossed it to one side of the road.

"I'll check on supper," he told us.

We watched him walk off, a bowlegged ramble older men seemed to aquire after time on horseback. He may have been a city slicker in his youth, but retirement must have been ten years behind him. Ten years on a broadback mare could make a person walk like that.

"You don't ride horses," Bem said from behind me.

I turned to see Bem, the Boy and Bis lined up shoulder to shoulder, all touching as if to reassure themselves they were really there.

My heart lurched in joy and fear. They were safe. They were here. It was all worth it. Every scar, every hurt, every person who stood in my way, gone, shot and not quite forgotten. Worth it.

"I could be a cowboy," I said. "Yee haw."

"I think it's yippi-kay-yay," the Boy smirked.

"You forgot the MF," Bis added.

"Language," I scolded with a smile. "I'm going to help out."

"We could help too," said the Boy.

"Help me by staying here," I stopped short of telling them to sit on the porch and wait.

Teens and pre-teens were not so good at sitting still and waiting for their parent to return from the wild.

"What are we going to do?" Bem asked.

"Chores," said Bis. "I'll show you."

She had spent her time as a ranch hand for months.

Bem asked the million dollar question as Brian walked up.

"Are we going to stay here?"

Bis nodded, before I could answer, but didn't say anything out loud.

The truth was, I hadn't decided.

And they were looking to me to decide. That weight was mine, somehow.

But there was too much to learn here still. Too much to see. About Meroni. About the world around us on the middle edge of Florida, tucked between the Space Coast and Orlando.

Part of the reason I wanted to ride with the man tomorrow was to learn more.

"I'll tell you when I know," I promised.

"It's safe," said Bis.

Safe was important. Especially for here and what she went through. What they all went through.

If it was true, we would stay.

If I could make it safer, I would.

23

CHAPTER TWENTY THREE

Don't you feel anything said Peg.

Her eyes were full of mist and regret, her voice crackling with tension.

How do you tell someone the truth about something like that?

That yes, I felt a lot, too much.

That losing my marriage and losing my children twice almost broke me, that watching another man raise them did break me.

That every day of my life was spent waiting for every other weekend and the twenty-four days a month alone took their toll.

The feelings wouldn't stop, the anger and regret and crushing loneliness night after night sent me into booze and between the legs of strangers just to feel loved for a moment. Or if not loved then wanted.

Just for the night and sometimes only for a few hours.

I turned to running be a useful it purged the feelings and I ran farther and farther until I felt nothing but the pain.

And still it didn't hurt half so bad as the loneliness, the emptiness.

"He feels," Anna said, her hand snaking through my arm.

The weight of it was comfortable and familiar and natural. I clenched my arm and cinched her tighter to me.

She sighed and pressed into me.

"He doesn't have to show it."

"I'm not asking him to start spouting Shakespeare," Peg said. "It'd be nice if he had a plan."

There it was.

One day back and she wanted me to fix a problem.

To tap into the one emotion I let them see, the one thing that I let them define me by.

Rage.

24

CHAPTER TWENTY FOUR

I punted him in the nuts.

All the crap about fair fighting was good for the boxing ring, where the rule was no hitting below the belt. In real life, it was better to crush nut butter out of a man's sack.

He fell over and puked.

That's how you know it's done right.

Tears streaming from his eyes, no way to breath, snot and slobber leaking out as he gaped on the floor, both hands cradled around his groin.

Which left his head free.

I played kick ball with the base of his skull. Not too hard, just a tap. Enough to snap his head forward so hard, his chin bounced off his sternum.

He bit through the tip of his tongue and the tiny piece of pink meat plopped out on the floor.

He still couldn't breathe to scream. He squirmed instead. Rolled, hands cupping his balls, trying to find safety.

There wasn't any.

I sent a second kick into this stomach, hard enough to jolt the diaphragm and took no pleasure as he fought against the spasms.

Mouth moving like a fish out of water. Open, shut. Open, shut.

It takes a lot to break some men. It depends on will. Their self reliance and pain tolerance. All of it was bullshit. All of it was training.

But some things come natural. Spend your whole life with the heart outside of the body, then tell me about pain.

Pieces of you scattered across the country. Other men raising your children as their own. Reading to them. Kissing their boo boo's.

And know it's all on you.

Your fault. Your choices. The dumb things you did and chose.

Spend a few nights in the cups, feeling that and then I'll tell you a story about pain.

Knowing you're not enough.

Will never be.

It took a minute to get control. To let go of his throat.

And by that time, he couldn't tell me anything.

Wouldn't be telling any anything again.

His wide eyes stared at me. An accusation. Judgement.

And I still didn't have the answers I needed.

25

CHAPTER TWENTY FIVE

"Dad!" she screamed.

Bis hit my chest with her knees and rode me down, straddling my arms.

I watched as she flicked open a lock blade with one hand and carved out my scratched eyeball with a deft twist of her wrist.

I had a moment of pure vision out of the one eye I had left, a phantom picture painted on my brain by the last time in my life I would ever have two eyes.

Then the pain hit.

I tried not to buck her off.

I clenched everything I had, every muscle, every cell and bit back a scream.

"Give me something to pack the socket," I heard her say.

I could feel blood guzzling down my cheek, clogging my ear.

"Open your eye Dad," she told me.

"You just cut my eye out," I said.

It wasn't easy with gritted teeth.

"Your eyelid," she sniffed.

And the trauma of it, the sheer ridiculousness of my twelve year old hacking out my Z scratched eyeball, then laughing when I corrected her about opening my eye lid hit me.

I giggled.

It was manic. I know.

It was partly a sob.

I could tell that too.

I heard her cry, felt the tears warm and wet on my cheeks.

At least I hoped they were tears.

"Is your nose dripping on me Bis?"

She laughed, and I stopped squinting. I could hear the Boy and Bem crying too, sniffling, and giggling.

It was messed up, sure, but a messed up situation called for screwed up responses.

She pulled my eyelid open.

"Hold it," she told Bem.

I felt her cool fingers against my skin.

Then Bis gently covered my eye socket with a dirty bandana.

"This will do for now," she said.

"That's going to get infected," Bem told us. "We need to get clean gauze, alcohol, antibiotics."

I held up a hand and they got quiet.

Then I opened the one eye I had left and sat up.

Bis had nose dripped on me.

I wiped off my cheek and showed it to her.

"Gross," I said softly.

She sobbed and punched her head into my chest, wrapped her arms around me and squeezed. Then the Boy and Bem were there too and my arms weren't big enough.

I held on as long as they would let me.

"You need to watch me," I said when they let go.

I pulled the pistol out of my belt and looked at it.

"If I start to turn, if it got in my system, I'm going to take care of it. But I need to get you safe first."

There was another round of sobbing.

But the kids were pragmatic. It was a new world, and this was a new solution, and there was no way in bloody hell I was making one of my kid's shoot their zombie dad.

Bem and the Boy had to do it to their mom.

Bis had to do it to her step-dad.

I'd take the samurai way out when it came to that.

First, there was business to attend.

"We need to find the others," I said. "Get back to them, and then make the plan."

I let them help me up. It made them feel better, and I didn't admit to them that I probably needed it.

This was going to take time to process.

I'd made it half way across the country, and back again. Fought milita. Religious cults. Meglomaniacs. And a couple of thousand zombies, maybe more.

Been shot. Been hurt. But never been bit.

I guess it was just the odds.

If you play with fire long enough, you're going to get burned.

I needed a cold beer.

The kids and I walked back toward the camp. Bem and Bis each under an arm, the Boy at point guarding us.

We weren't laughing anymore.

26

CHAPTER TWENTY SIX

I stopped us at the edge of the marina.

"I've always wanted a boat," I mused.

"Dad!" the Boy snapped. "No."

"What? I think it's a great idea. We take a boat, sail along the coast. No Z can get to us, no soldiers, nobody. We can drift in the gulfstream current or make sails. It's a great idea."

"Seriously Dad?" Bis snickered. "A one-eyed man in a boat?"

"I can see well enough."

"He doesn't get it," said Bem.

I didn't.

Whatever they were trying to tell me, I didn't understand.

"I don't see what you're saying," I pointed to the patch covering my eye.

"You'd be a pirate, Dad," the Boy sighed. "All you would be missing is saying argh."

"Arr?"

"Argh."

"Yar?"

"Argh."

"Yar is a sailing term, but maybe we could apply it to a yacht. And I wouldn't make you call me the Dread Pirate Robert, unless you really wanted to. Then I wouldn't stop you."

"The Dread Pirate Robert? That's not your name," said my youngest.

"It's much more terrifying than the Dread Pirate Wesley."

They looked at me, six eyes, all gorgeous brown and beautiful and wise beyond their years. Not one crinkled in a smile or lit up in recognition.

"What did your mother's teach you?" I sighed. "Have you never heard of the Princess Bride? Come on, let's go get a boat."

"As you wish," Bem said and we all broke out in laughter.

THE END

9 798822 364548 1